Level 4 is ideal for cl[...]
read longer texts with c[...]
are eager to start readi[...]

Special features:

Full
exploration
of subject

vocabulary

The emergent layer
Many animals that live in the emergent layer fly, jump or glide. Macaws look for fruit and plants to eat.

Macaws nest in here.

This eagle has big claws. It hunts monkeys, sloths and snakes in the trees.

Central America
South America

14

15

Detailed
illustrations
capture the
imagination

Longer sentences

On the ground
Ants make big nests on the damp forest floor. Anteaters dig into the nest with their claws to get the ants.

Central America
South America

Fruit rots and is eaten by beetles.

Big spiders live on the ground.

Worm lizards hunt in the leaves.

Captions
offer further
explanation

Educational Consultant: Geraldine Taylor
Book Banding Consultant: Kate Ruttle
Subject Consultant: Steve Parker

LADYBIRD BOOKS

UK | USA | Canada | Ireland | Australia
India | New Zealand | South Africa

Ladybird Books is part of the Penguin Random House group of companies
whose addresses can be found at global.penguinrandomhouse.com.

www.penguin.co.uk www.puffin.co.uk www.ladybird.co.uk

Penguin
Random House
UK

First published 2018
005

Copyright © Ladybird Books Ltd, 2018

Printed in China

A CIP catalogue record for this book is available from the British Library

ISBN: 978–0–241–31257–5

All correspondence to
Ladybird Books
Penguin Random House Children's Books
One Embassy Gardens, 8 Viaduct Gardens, London SW11 7BW

Rainforests

Written by Zoë Clarke
Illustrated by Galia Bernstein

Contents

Tropical rainforests

This is a tropical rainforest. Tropical rainforests grow where it is very hot and there is lots of sun and rain.

The Amazon Rainforest is the largest tropical rainforest on Earth.

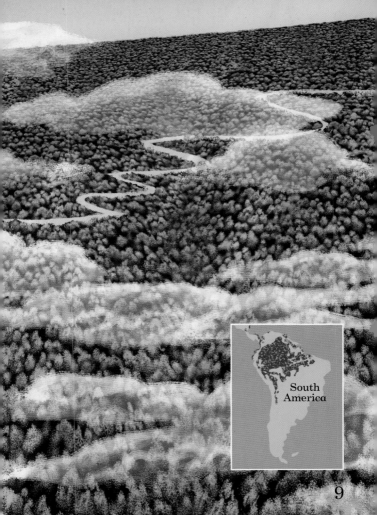

South America

Where on Earth?

Here are all the tropical rainforests on Earth.

Central America

South America

Half of all the animal and plant species on Earth live in rainforests.

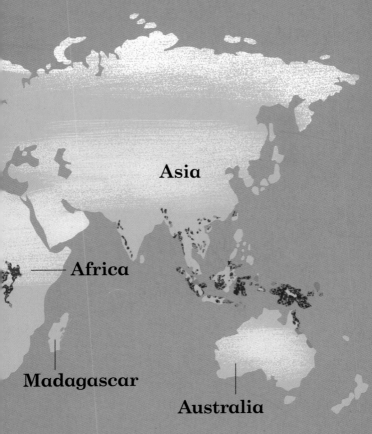

Asia

—— Africa

Madagascar

Australia

Rainforest layers

Tropical rainforests have different layers.

Emergent – lots of sun and rain up here

Canopy – very hot here

Understorey – warm, dark and damp here

Forest floor – very dark and very damp down here

13

The emergent layer

Many animals that live in the emergent layer fly, jump or glide. Macaws look for fruit and plants to eat.

Macaws nest in here.

This eagle has big claws. It hunts monkeys, sloths and snakes in the trees.

Central America

South America

Jumping monkeys

These capuchin monkeys live in the emergent layer. They jump around, using their tails to climb. They eat fruit, insects, frogs and lizards.

16

Capuchin monkeys have to look out for eagles!

South America

17

People in the rainforest

In some tropical rainforests, people make their homes in the treetops with the animals.

This home is away from the danger of other people and big animals. There is only one way up . . . and one way down!

Asia

In the canopy

Howler monkeys are the loudest monkeys in the forest. They can be heard almost five kilometres away!

Central America

South America

Howler monkeys and orangutans live in different rainforests, but they both live in the canopy, and eat leaves and fruit.

Jump or climb?

This big lizard lives in the canopy. It jumps to get away from other animals. If the lizard's tail comes off, it can grow back!

Central America

South America

Sloths do not jump. Sloths climb slowly through the canopy with their big claws. They eat leaves and fruit slowly, too.

Central America

South America

Understorey layer

Bats, birds and insects live down in the warm, damp understorey layer.

A praying mantis eats a beetle.

Central / America

South America

Africa

Asia

Australia

Some bats live by the water and hunt fish.

Central
America

South
America

The Amazon River
Caimans can grow very big.
They live in the water and on land.

South
America

Piranhas hunt in the Amazon River. They are small but can eat big animals like caimans.

These snakes eat caimans, too!

Big river animals

These river otters live around the Amazon River. They eat lots of fish.

Some otters grow very big!

Manatees live in the water. They
swim slowly, and eat river plants.

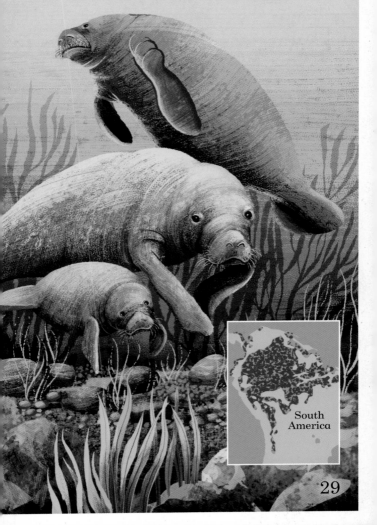

South
America

Forest floor

It is very dark and damp on the forest floor. Forest elephants look for leaves and fruit here.

Africa

In a different rainforest, lemurs jump down from the understorey to hunt for fruit on the forest floor.

Madagascar

Big cats

Big cats, like jaguars, live on the forest floor. Jaguars hunt monkeys, sloths and caimans. They can swim, and they eat fish.

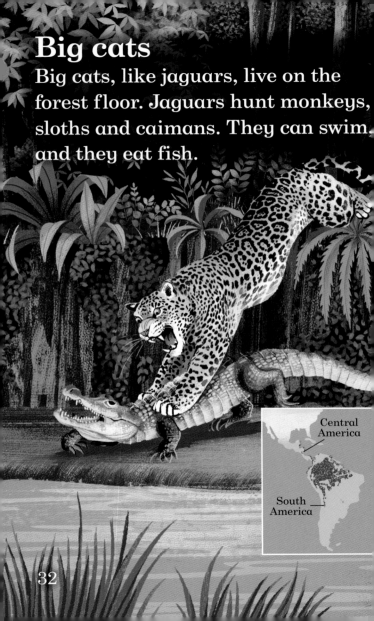

Central America

South America

Tigers live on the forest floor of a different rainforest. Here, they swim in rivers.

Asia

On the ground

Ants make big nests on the damp forest floor. Anteaters dig into the nest with their claws to get the ants.

Central America

South America

Fruit rots and is eaten by beetles.

Big spiders live on the ground.

Worm lizards hunt in the leaves.

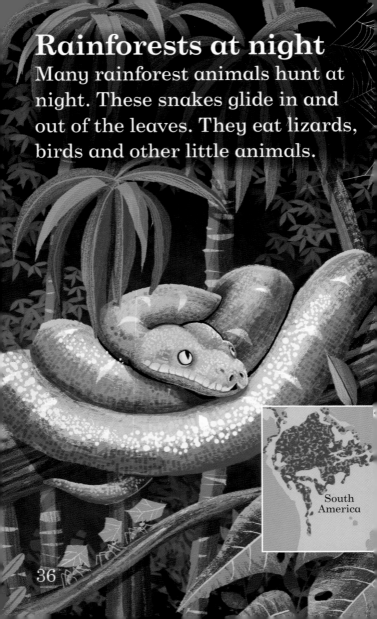

Rainforests at night

Many rainforest animals hunt at night. These snakes glide in and out of the leaves. They eat lizards, birds and other little animals.

South America

Tree frogs hunt insects and other little frogs.

Central America

South America

Glow in the dark

Trees rot on the forest floor, and this is where fungi grow. In many rainforests, the fungi glow at night.

These beetles glow at night, too!

Central America

South America

Rainforests in danger

Plant and animal species in the tropical rainforests are in danger.

People take the trees away, and then many animals have no homes.

Can we get the tropical rainforests back?

We can get the tropical rainforests back, but we must not take away any more trees.

Growing more trees helps the rainforests.

42

We must help make new homes for the different species of animals.

We all have to help, or the rainforests will be gone.

Picture glossary

 anteaters

 capuchin monkeys

 claws

 eagle

 fungi

 howler monkeys